This book is by
Alex T. Smith and

Eva Kernigan

If lost please return.

✗ (juicy bone baguette reward) ✗

D1637808

This book is for all of Claude and
Sir Bobblysock's lovely fans (that means YOU!)
Happy doodling!

Hodder Children's Books
An imprint of Hachette Children's Group. Part of Hodder & Stoughton.
Carmelite House, 50 Victoria Embankment, London EC4Y 0DZ

An Hachette UK Company
www.hachette.co.uk

CLAUDE

Doodle Book

ALEX T. SMITH and ....

← Put your name here

Hodder Children's Books

An imprint of Hachette Children's Group

How to Draw Claude

You will need: a pencil, a red pencil, a biscuit.

Claude is a small, plump dog who wears a fancy beret and a stylish red sweater. Can you draw him?

Step 1

Step 2

Step 3

Step 4

Step 5

Step 6

Now eat the biscuit

Best Friends

Claude's best friend is Sir Bobblysock,
who is both a sock and quite bobbly.
Design your own clothing sidekick.

Don't forget to give your pal some accessories. Bow tie? Sunglasses? Snazzy specs?

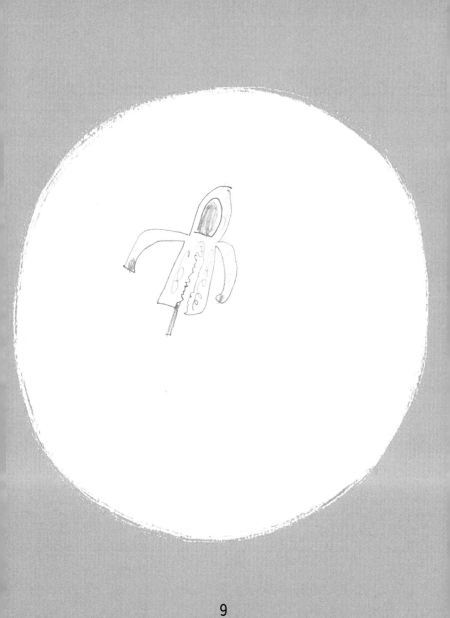

Mr and Mrs
Shinyshoes

Add their snazzy outfits here

Claude lives with Mr and Mrs Shinyshoes.
Every day they dash out of the door to work.
What will they wear today? You decide!

Meet Claude in the City

Claude loves to explore in the city. He has noticed there are lots of pigeons around. Can you draw some other things he might spot?

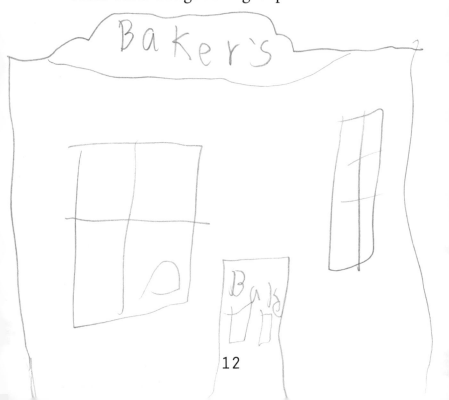

Park Life

On a sunny day, Claude loves to have fun in the park! Design your own play park for Claude.

Don't forget to add Sir Bobblysock
enjoying an ice cream!

Beret Boutique

Claude LOVES wearing his beret, but he's keen to try some new hats. Can you design some splendid ones for him?

17

Super Signs

Design your own
shop signs.

the
1 * Harry
potter
shop

magic

Design Your Own Art Gallery

Claude is terribly interested in this nice statue. Can you draw some more objects on the plinths to look at?

Create Your Own Masterpieces

Stop Thief!

Uh-oh! This naughty robber has stolen something. What's in her hand? You decide!

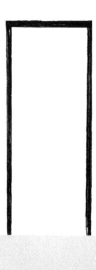

It could be a large painting or a teeny-tiny jewel.

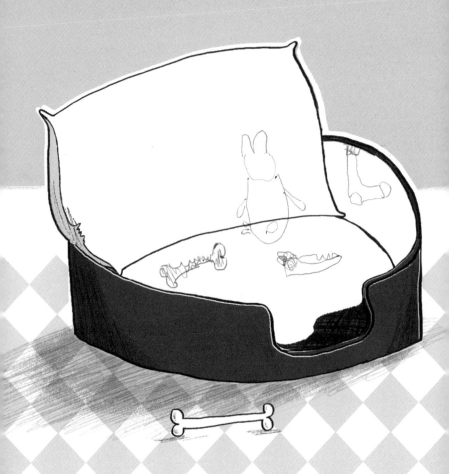

Claude's Basket

Claude's friends need a nap. Can you draw them all tucked up in bed?

Dr Chewed Squeakybone

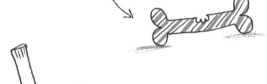

Mr Smelly Sock

Dame Nibbled-Slipper

Keith

Can You Draw Some New Friends for Claude?

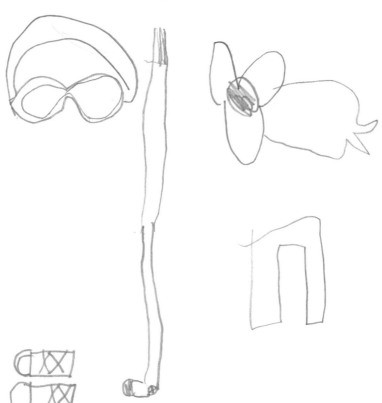

Fill this whole page with **new** chums.

29

Claude at the Seaside

Design Claude's snazzy swimwear.

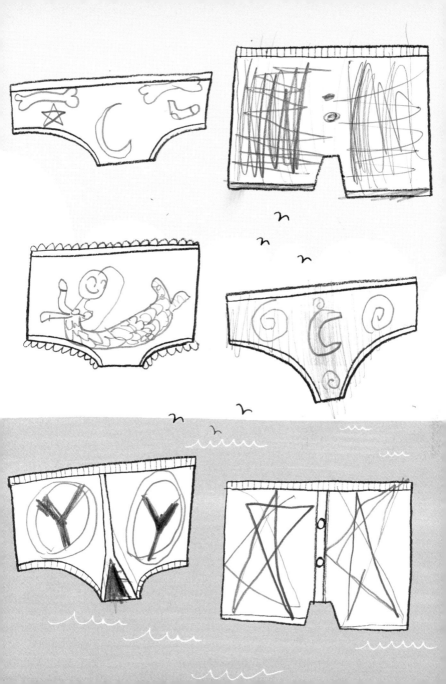

Dear...

Fill in these postcards, pretending you are on holiday with Claude.

Hey Look at my Art could we have a Play, may be a sleep over

Why not send it to your best friend?

Draw yourself with **Claude** at the seaside.

33

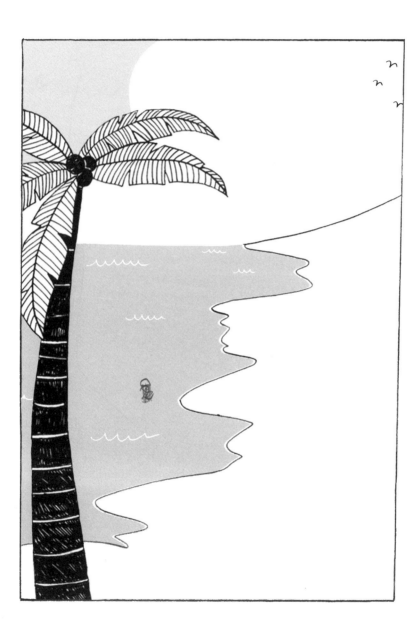

Claude on Holiday

Claude is learning to say 'hello' in lots of different languages.

Bonjour

(French)

Konnichiwa

(Japanese)

Hola

(Spanish)

Woof

(Dog)

Do you know any other ways to say hello?

Gooddai Mate (Australia)

Hallo (German)

Halloe (English)

37

Sandcastle Competition

Sir Bobblysock has made a giant sandcastle. Can you design an even bigger one?

39

Porthole Pete

This is Claude's friend Porthole Pete.
Can you draw some more pirate chums?

Why not draw your friends or family as pirates?

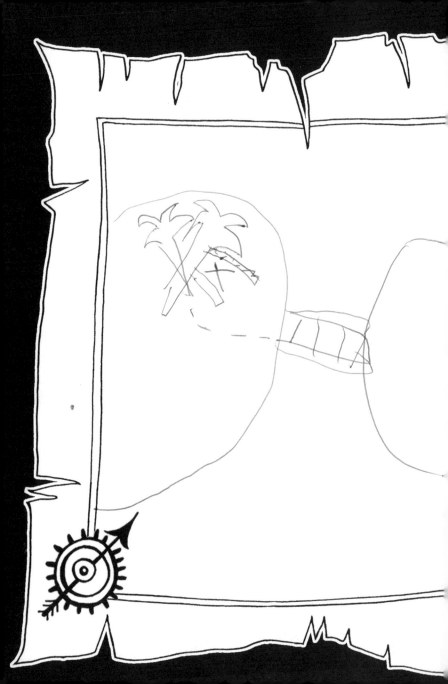

Create your own treasure island map. Don't forget to draw an X where the treasure is hidden.

44

Desert Island

Claude and Sir Bobblysock are marooned on a desert island. Luckily he has all the essentials to survive. Draw the things you would take with you!

Waggy
Avenue

Victer
Hogo

Anna's
Art
Palis

Claude loves to shop on Waggy Avenue. Name his favourite shops.

Claude's Costumes

Claude loves to rummage around
in his dressing-up box! Design your
own ravishing outfit for him.

49

Wig Wonder!

Claude is ever so partial to a good wig! Design your own lovely new hairdos for Claude.

GORILLA THRILLER

Movie Star

Claude once starred in a gorilla thriller.
Add his co-stars to this movie poster.

Claude in the Country

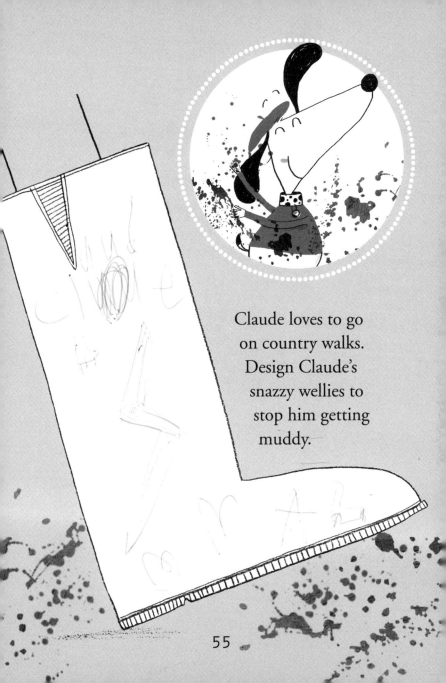

Claude loves to go
on country walks.
Design Claude's
snazzy wellies to
stop him getting
muddy.

Down on the Farm

Here we are on Mrs Cowpat's farm. Draw the animals who live here!

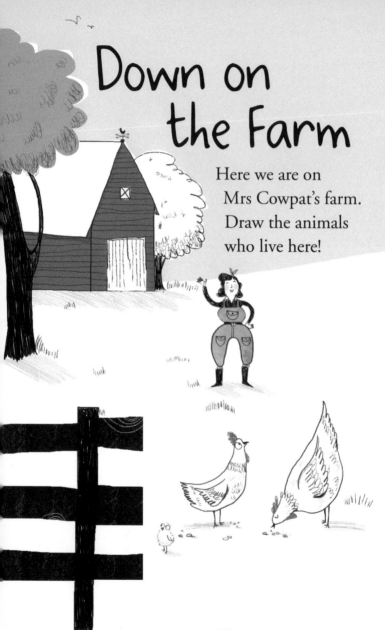

Mrs Cowpat's Tractor

Claude doesn't think Mrs Cowpat's tractor is snazzy enough. Can you decorate it for the country fair?

Use flags, balloons, bows and ribbons!

60

Most Beautiful Pigs Competition

Can you draw some more glamorous pigs getting ready for the Country Show?

Claude Loves to Dance

Can you give Claude a top hat
and cane, and add a dancing partner?

STOP
WHAT YOU ARE DOING IMMEDIATELY AND HAVE A SNACK!

Doodling is very hard work. You deserve a treat. Draw your favourite snack here.

Proten bar

Dance-Off!

Learn how to dance like Claude.

1. Leg kick

2. Wiggle

3. Bottom shake

4. Jump

5. Spin

67

Keep on Dancing!

Can you add some more dance moves for Claude?

6. Ponytail fick

7. Worm

8. spin

9. Sholder twist

Don't forget, Claude is an expert at ear waggling!

Spooky Time

Every theatre has a ghost or two. Can you draw some spooky ghosts here? They are probably up to something a bit naughty.

Claude at the Circus

Claude has joined the circus.
Design his snazzy clown trousers
and give him a red nose!

Roll Up! Roll Up!

Design your own circus poster starring Claude and Sir Bobblysock, of course!

The best
Come to the circus

WOW

Yay

come on!!!

Claude's Favourite Jokes

What kind of dog takes a bubble bath?

A shampoodle!

What swings from a trapeze and miaows?

An acrocat!

Why do dogs
wag their tails?

Because no one
will do it for them!

Add your
favourite
jokes here

What is a vampires
favrite fruite?

blood Orange

Knock Knock
who's there
docter
docter who
you ruined my joke

Detective Story

One morning, Claude and Sir

Bobblysock's tummies were making

grumpy, grumbly noises. They decided

what they each needed was a lovely

cake from Mr Lovelybuns' Bakery.

But when they got to the shop, they

discovered Mr Lovelybuns was in an

awful tizz!

'Someone has stolen the big,

beautiful birthday cake I just

finished icing. It was in the

window, and now it isn't!' he cried.

This sounded very much like a case

for Claude the Detective to solve.

So he whipped his magnifying glass

out from under his beret, and he and

Sir Bobblysock set to work. First

the two friends. looked for crums

Remember to make sure something really exciting happens in the middle of your story!

Will Claude and Sir Bobblysock solve the crime?

The End

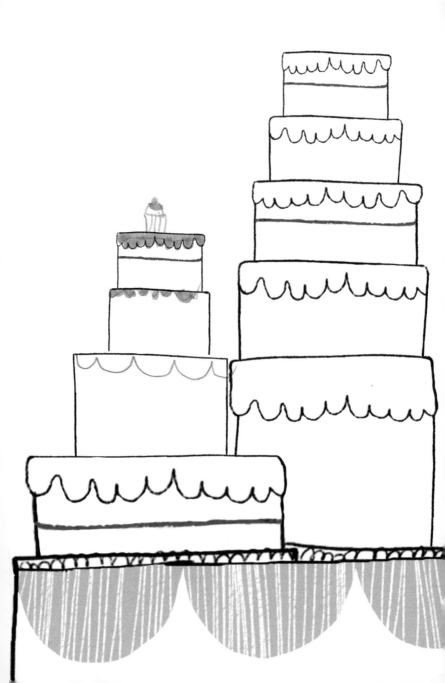

Claude Loves Cakes

Can you help Claude make these cakes look as yummy and as bonkers as possible?

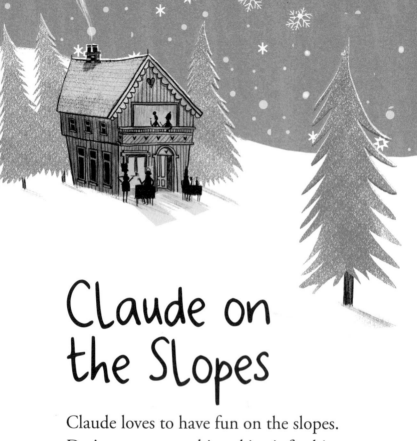

Claude on the Slopes

Claude loves to have fun on the slopes.
Design an eye-catching ski suit for him.

Why not add stripes, spots or zig-zags?

Claude's Binoculars

Uh-oh! Claude's spotted something. Can you draw the surprising thing he's seen?

Great Snowman Competition

Enter the competition and design your own snowman.

The Marvellous Marvin

Claude loves to impress
the Marvellous Marvin, a
world-famous magician, with
his tricks. What has Claude
conjured up from
his hat today?

Remember to draw Claude's glamorous assistant (Sir Bobblysock).

93

Giant Vegetable Competition

Enter the competition and design
your own prize-winning vegetable!

Musical Claude

Claude loves to bang, crash and honk!
Create your own one-man band.

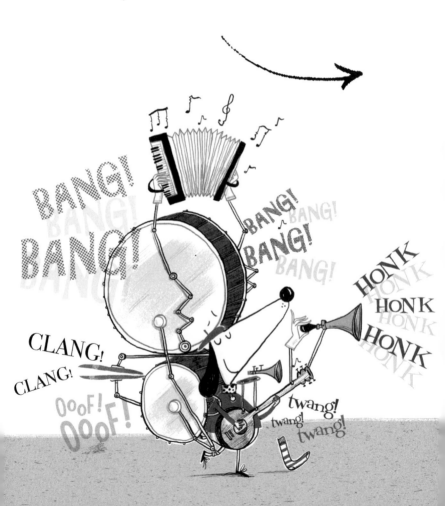

Claude's Pets

Draw yourself with your favourite pets.

Bounce With Claude!

On a nothing-to-do-day Claude loves to bounce on a trampoline. Can you draw yourself bouncing with Claude and Sir Bobblysock?

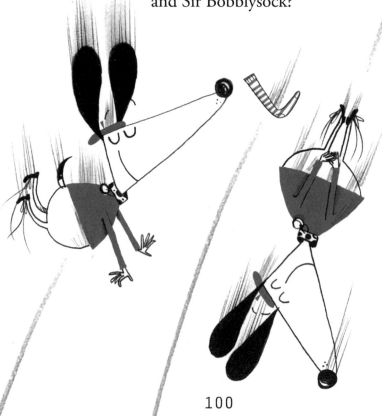

Washing Day!

Claude has given his beret a jolly good spring clean and has hung all the things he stores in there on the line. What has he been keeping under his hat?

Remember to **draw** Claude's favourite **juicy bone** baguette.

Interesting Films

Claude loves watching cowboy films.
Can you draw Claude and Sir Bobblysock
in an exciting cowboy scene?

Sir Bobblysock's Snooze

It's time for Sir Bobblysock to have one of his Long Lie-Downs. Write down all the things he needs for a good kip.

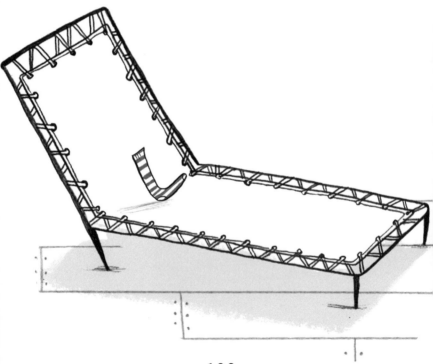

1. Cucumber slices for his eyes

2. His cardigan

3.

4.

5.

6.

7.

8.

Have you **read** these **books** about Claude?

Which is your favourite and why?

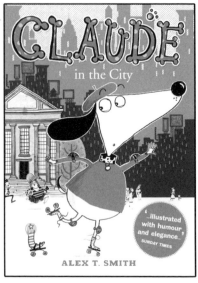

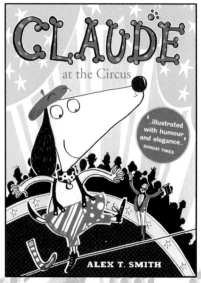

CLAUDE in the Country

'...illustrated with humour and elegance...' SUNDAY TIMES

ALEX T. SMITH

CLAUDE in the Spotlight

'...illustrated with humour and elegance...' SUNDAY TIMES

ALEX T. SMITH

CLAUDE on the Slopes

'...illustrated with humour and elegance...' SUNDAY TIMES

ALEX T. SMITH

CLAUDE Lights! Camera! Action!

'...illustrated with humour and elegance...' SUNDAY TIMES

ALEX T. SMITH

Where Next?

Where will you send Claude and
Sir Bobblysock on their next adventure?
Can you create some covers for new stories?

Remember to put your name here

CLAUDE

CLAUDE

CLAUDE

Goodbye From Claude

Claude has had lots of doodling fun with you. Can you sign your name and say goodbye too?

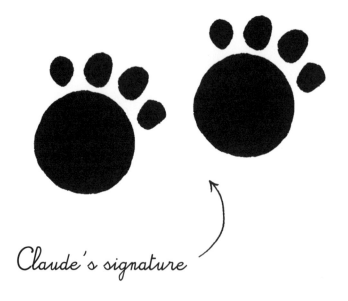

Claude's signature

Your signature

This page is blank for you to fill with doodles.

This page is blank for you to fill with doodles.

This page is blank for you to fill with doodles.

This page is blank for you to fill with doodles.

Alex T. Smith graduated from university in 2006 with a degree in illustration. His favourite hobbies are people-watching, eavesdropping and being a world-class window-looker-outer. He works under the supervision of three very tiny, naughty dogs.

Draw yourself here with your favourite pet and write your own biography.